For Katie Molles

A Silly Story

Written and illustrated by Mercer Mayer

GINGHAM DOG
PRESS

Columbus, Ohio

Children's Publishing

Text © 1972 Mercer Mayer
Illustrations © 1972 Mercer Mayer
Cover Illustrations © 1972 Mercer Mayer

This edition published in the United States of America in 2003 by
Gingham Dog Press
an imprint of McGraw-Hill Children's Publishing,
a Division of The McGraw-Hill Companies
8787 Orion Place
Columbus, Ohio 43240-4027

www.MHkids.com

Library of Congress Cataloging-in-Publication Data on file with the publisher.

 A Big Tuna Trading Company, LLC/J.R. Sansevere Book

Printed in The United States of America.

1-57768-338-2

1 2 3 4 5 6 7 8 9 10 PHXBK 08 07 06 05 04 03 02

The McGraw·Hill Companies

Once I had a silly thought
while sitting in the shade.

What if I'm not me.
Perhaps I am a rock,
a dog, or a tree,
thinking I am me...
What a silly thought.

I laughed so hard I fell
right down and then
I thought some more.

Perhaps each time
I smell a flower,
it is smelling me right back.

Perhaps I'm not where
I think I am.
Where else can I be?
Sitting in a tree?

Or hiding underneath a stone.

And what if I'm floating
high up in the air
and I only think that
I am sitting in the shade.

Perhaps up is down and
down is up and I only
think it's down.

That silly thinking
made me hungry
so I went home to eat.

My dinner lay there
on the plate,
looking up at me.
Then I had a silly thought.

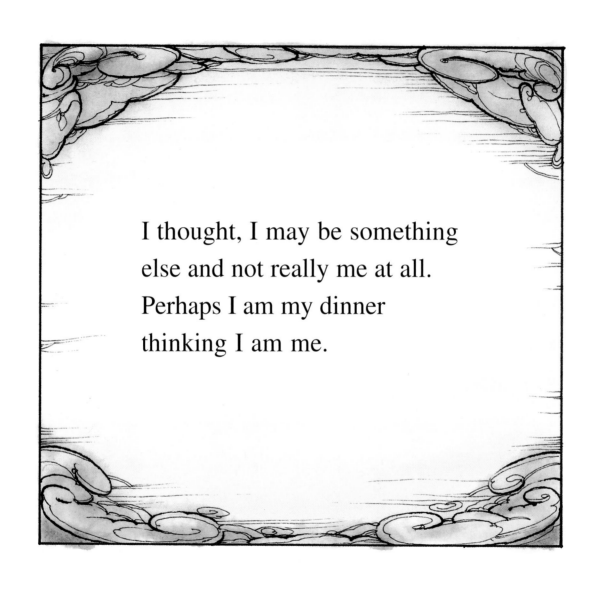

I thought, I may be something
else and not really me at all.
Perhaps I am my dinner
thinking I am me.

That made me laugh
so very hard
I fell right off my chair.

"Eat your dinner,"
my father said.
"Why must you be so silly?"

Maybe I'm not here at all.

Where else can I be?

Perhaps I'm under the tablecloth.

And I just don't know

I'm there.

"Stop that now,"
my mother said,
"and go upstairs to bed."

I put on my pajamas
and crawled into my bed.
Before I knew what happened
I had a silly thought.

Perhaps I am my pillow
and my pillow
is really me.

That made me laugh
so very hard
I fell right out of bed.

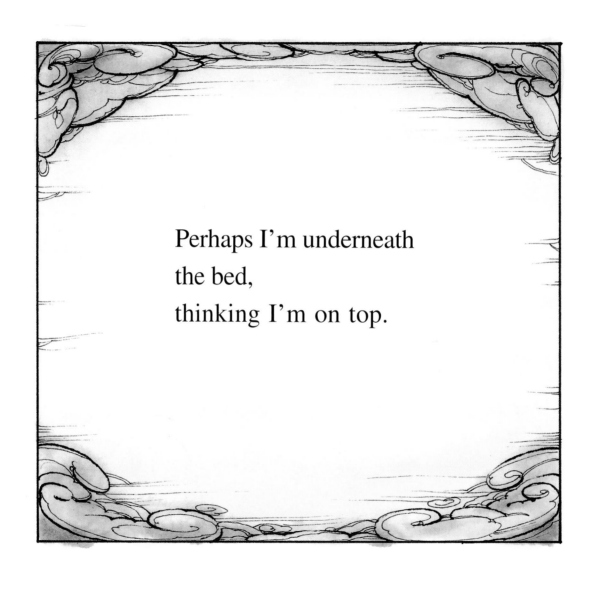

Perhaps I'm underneath
the bed,
thinking I'm on top.

All those silly thoughts
running through my head
made me very tired
so I closed my eyes.
While I had my eyes closed
I had a silly thought.

I don't remember
what it was because
I fell asleep.